# ALTERATIONS

# BOOKS BY JANE SUEN

*Children of the Future*
*Flowers in December*
*Alterations*

# ALTERATIONS

JANE SUEN

Jane Suen books are available for order through Ingram Press Catalogues

www.janesuen.com

Printed in the United States of America

First Printing: July 2017

ISBN: 978-0-9979297-5-1

Ebook ISBN: 978-0-9979297-4-4

*For my family and friends.*

# Chapter 1
## GIGI

Gigi revved the engine of her old, trusty car. She cranked the window down halfway. Backbone straight, she adjusted her grip on the steering wheel. She focused, bent on reaching her destination, setting her sight on it like a bullseye, having practiced this a million times in her mind—visualizing this moment, every second in slow motion, her mind obsessed with it.

She took one last look in the rearview mirror, fixing her hair and touching up her lipstick. *A girl's gotta look good on this special day.* She had picked the spot. No negotiating or backing out now.

Taking in a deep breath, she held it for a brief second, then let it out with a satisfying *swoosh.*

If her hands were free, she would have been pummeling her chest like Tarzan and making that high-pitched, savage cry. She smiled, picturing Tarzan swinging across treetops, traveling with exhilarating speed on the canopy highway of the jungle. She allowed herself this final

1

indulgence before pressing on the gas pedal and speeding down the deserted highway, heading straight toward the concrete wall of the curved underpass.

She tightened her grip on the wheel one more time.

At the last moment, an instant before the crash, the wall looming, Gigi's survival instinct kicked in. The tires screeched. Then metal scratched concrete, scraping the front corner and the left side of the car, ripping off the side mirror as she turned the wheel in a desperate attempt to save herself, the car careening one way, then jerking back, before coming to an abrupt stop on the grassy strip on the other side of the highway. The car fizzed as it expelled its final breaths.

# Chapter 2

## DR. KITE

A white van pulled up beside the car and two men jumped out, rolling a gurney. They put Gigi, still unconscious, on the stretcher. One man went back to grab her purse, scooping up the contents which spilled in his hurry. He looked around, eyes darting everywhere, keeping a wary watch on the road for vehicles. The other, a taller man, checked her pulse before placing a call on his cell phone.

"We found her." He listened and nodded. "Uh-huh… through the tracking device in her microchip… we're on our way."

The van sped away, leaving no trace. It raced into the city and to a warehouse docking area, disappearing into the dark hollows of the building as the doors swung closed behind it.

The two men wheeled Gigi into a room where a man dressed in medical scrubs was waiting. With his stereoscopic eyepiece, he could be mistaken for a dentist.

"Dr. Kite, she's all yours," the taller man said. He watched as the doctor carefully examined Gigi, then made a slit in her upper arm, removing a microchip encased in a clear capsule.

"What have I done?" said the doctor as he stared at the chip.

# Chapter 3

## DR. KITE

Gigi had never been suicidal before. Her death wish, propelling her toward an extremely violent end, only came after he implanted this new mind control chip. Did it malfunction, triggering an out-of-character suicide attempt?

Kite looked at Gigi stretched out on the table. *We gave you perfection, how could you not want that? No disease, no malfunctioning organs, every cell optimized and in perfect working order.*

And she would never have to worry as long as the microchip was inside her. She was a lucky one. Every healthy cell programmed to copy and regenerate on a timetable, every sick cell targeted to die. It was his masterpiece.

He conducted hundreds of scientific experiments, working tirelessly until he successfully developed his products. Gigi had been implanted with one of his three earlier prototypes. That original microchip needed an enhancement, long overdue, so they called her in last week to implant a new second-generation, upgraded model with mind control and a tracking device.

If only, this time, they *could* control the mind. The body they could now fix—not just for cosmetic reasons, but to cure people who were ill like Gigi, destroying the defective cells and replacing them with healthy ones. Once he perfected this microchip, he would have riches beyond imagination. How many people? Millions, no *billions*. Why, he'd even offer different grades of this microchip to make it more affordable. He could almost hear the people clamoring for it.

He touched Gigi's face. She had been cleaned up, every trace of the near-crash removed. He sighed. The upgraded mind control chip he'd implanted—he had been so close to the ultimate success. But he wasn't there yet. What went wrong today? Had it tried to make Gigi do something against her nature? Did she suppress or override its mind control? Was the chip ineffective or defective? With a shrug, he turned, walked across the room to retrieve Gigi's original chip from storage, then re-implanted it in her arm.

The taller man wheeled Gigi down the hall and into a vast room filled with drawers. He slid her into an empty cabinet and rolled it shut. On the keypad next to it, he selected the "Regenerate" button.

# Chapter 4
## LILLY

They let Gigi sleep. And sleep well she did that night, undisturbed in the hard cocoon of her drawer, kept warm and quiet, accompanied by the soft hum of the equipment. Nothing was left to chance that might stand in the way of optimal recovery for Dr. Kite's patients. Especially Gigi. Tonight was a tough night, with Kite worrying about Gigi again. Her actions and movements were becoming more erratic since he implanted the new upgrade a few days ago. She wasn't as careful about making good choices, getting out of control. Something was going wrong with the new chip, so he'd secretly rescued her and healed her from the accident, because he didn't want her to know.

When he was in medical school, he was a bright-eyed idealist. He wanted to be the next great healer. He wasn't the most brilliant scientist in the world, but he had other talents—an astute mind that seized upon a chance discovery, and the drive and persistence to succeed. Before that, he had an interest in electrical engineering. After earning a bachelor's degree in that field, Kite worked as a test engineer in the wireless microchip and biomedical industries. His combined interest led him to this project. It took him twenty-two years to do it, to make changes, refine, improve, and test this new chip technology. *Now,* he thought, *it's close to the finish line.*

As he pulled out of the warehouse, Kite nodded to the guys. He could hear his mother's refined voice saying, "Be nice to everyone." Driving in the quiet of the evening relaxed him. What happened to Gigi shook him up. Needing time to think, unwind, and relieve some of the tension his body still carried from the day, he headed into the parking lot of Duggers—his favorite restaurant where he felt like, and was treated like, royalty.

"Good evening, doctor," said the hostess, flashing him a warm smile she reserved for special customers.

"Good to see you, Sally," said Kite. Leaning closer he murmured, "I, um… I've been busy and don't have a reservation for tonight. Perhaps you could get me a seat?"

"Your usual place?"

"Yes, please."

Sally picked up a menu and led the way to his table. She thought it was empty, but as she approached, it was clear a woman was sitting there, alone. Sally turned around, facing Kite. "Oh, I'm sorry…"

Kite glanced at the woman, fighting his disappointment. "That's all right. You can seat me at the other table."

Sally looked relieved but sought his assurance. "You're sure that's all right? I've never seen you at another table. This is your lucky table, as you always say," she gushed, a nervous squeak in her voice.

"Tonight is this lady's lucky night," Kite said with a gracious wave.

The woman at the table watched him. A trace of a smile flickered across her face.

He gave her the briefest nod, holding her glance for a moment longer.

"Well in that case, let me share my luck," the lady said. "Would you like to join me?"

Her invitation caught him by surprise. He was still ruffled, but his well-bred exterior betrayed no such thing. He gave a slight bow in thanks before extending his hand. "Dr. Kite, at your service."

"I'm Lilly Cooper." They shook hands.

"Ms. or Mrs., may I ask?" Kite said as he pulled back the chair to sit across from her.

"The former Mrs. Cooper. Perhaps you know my ex-husband, Frank Cooper?"

"I'm afraid not."

"He introduced me to this place. We used to come here often. It was popular in the day. It's farther now, since I've moved, but I still come here on occasion." She paused. "But Frank stopped coming," she added.

"I hope I'm not disturbing you."

"Oh no, not at all. I've had my peace and quiet while I enjoyed my meal. This is perfect timing—I've just ordered coffee and dessert."

"I don't believe I've seen you here," said Kite as he leaned forward and spoke with friendliness in his naturally deep voice, determined to have a good evening. "Today's *my* lucky day. I appreciate your generosity in sharing your table with me."

"I believe in luck, Dr. Kite," cooed Lilly. "I need all the luck I can get."

# Chapter 5

## GIGI

Gigi woke up with a slight headache. It was dark. She tried to remember where she was and what she was doing. She touched her face. Lying in the darkness, she reached out with her fingers to explore her surroundings. She pushed against a hard surface, feeling its smoothness. She panicked, thinking she was in a coffin. This can't be happening! *Calm down*, she chided herself.

Last night, Gigi had tossed and turned. Her body craved rest, but her mind stayed wired up, even knowing she was safe at home, in her own bedroom, on her bed. Her mind was running, trying to get away, fighting to stay awake, dreading the terrifying nightmare that had presented itself for a few nights in a row since she got the upgraded microchip. But, despite her efforts, she eventually fell into an uneasy rest. Something wasn't right.

She went over the events now, trying to recall, to bring back a memory. As hard as she tried, she couldn't remember. That irked her. Wanting to retrieve a piece of her memory which may be the key to unlocking the mystery of what happened, she closed her eyes to concentrate. She was in her car, checking herself in the rearview mirror. Sometime after that it became fuzzier. It had to be important. Racking her brain to think hurt.

She checked the rest of her body, reaching as far she could. She was all there, no missing parts or limbs. She wiggled her toes and moved her legs and arms. To be sure, she pinched herself. *Ouch.* Sure felt that.

Bits and pieces flashed in front of her eyes—the looming concrete wall, the interior of her car, her foot slamming on the brake, the loud screeching, and then nothing more. Well, something must have happened, but she didn't die. Was she in a car accident? A fender bender? But she wasn't in pain, and she wasn't hurting. No broken bones. *Now c'mon Gigi, think. Try and remember as much as you can.* She vaguely recalled someone looking at her, soft murmurs, and being transported in a vehicle.

So what was this place? There didn't seem to be a latch of any kind on the inside she could push or pull. She could hear something whirling. Gigi strained, hoping to gain a clue of her whereabouts. Relief flooded her as she realized she didn't die in fiery flames or an injury so bad that inflicted broken bones, crushed vital organs, or left her paralyzed. What had she been doing? She was determined to find the answers.

As Gigi pondered what to do next, she heard a spraying sound and felt a cooling mist. In a panic, she pushed hard, trying to get out, fearful of being gassed to death. There was nowhere to escape. Gigi put her hand over her mouth, pinched her nose, and held her breath. But that didn't work. The mist began filling the space, covering her, and she finally succumbed to sleep, a deep slumber.

Her body regenerated, cell by cell.

# Chapter 6

## DR. KITE

When morning came, Kite was up early, a habit he had acquired during his early years in medical school when he worked long days and was on call through the night. Sleeping late was a luxury he only allowed himself on rare occasions, even to this day. He had received a text during the night and approved the administration of a mist to help Gigi sleep as her body regenerated overnight. It was in her best interest. Anxious to see her, he rushed back at the break of dawn.

Kite smiled. Today was turning out better than he ever imagined. As soon as he arrived, he checked on Gigi. If they hadn't gotten to her within minutes, she may have died from her injuries. She was lucky to be alive and under his watchful eye. The microchip he'd inserted last night, her original one, appeared to work fine. Satisfied with her quick recovery through the night, he approved her release. He made final preparations, calculating how much time remained before she'd wake up. Then he summoned the two men who had brought her in yesterday.

They worked efficiently, putting Gigi back in the white van along with her purse and driving to a hotel parking deck nearby. They half-dragged her into the elevator and hit the button for the lobby floor. As soon as the elevator doors opened, they propped an almost-awake Gigi between their arms and carried her to a chair out of sight of the security cameras. In the few minutes remaining before she woke up, they made her comfortable while standing in front of her, blocking any inquisitive glances. The timing was perfect, the crowd of guests checking out keeping the hotel staff busy. The taller man made a call to Kite.

The doctor was in fabulous spirits. He called himself a doctor, but if anybody checked, they wouldn't be able to find his medical degree or license. In truth, Kite didn't even finish medical school. He dropped out midway through his fourth year. In his mind, he was still a doctor, and thought he had every right to call himself one. Nobody had ever questioned him, or his credentials. In his white coat, he exuded authority and confidence.

He passed by the monitor room. All the lights were green, the rows of screens lit up, one for each of the sleeping bodies in the cabinets, the new people brought in each night. The next morning, they'd be rotated out, released back to the world once he'd examined them. These were people they found passed out on sidewalks, lost travelers—anyone not likely to be missed for a few hours.

They had a fake taxicab that trawled the city at night, picking up rides. But as a rule, only single passengers. Most of the time, the riders were too drunk or high to be aware of what was happening. They could barely talk or walk. The overnight stay was just a precaution, in case of an adverse reaction to the microchip. If that occurred, then Kite would remove it. The person was released, and nobody was any the wiser.

# Chapter 7
## GIGI

When Gigi didn't come home, Rex was up all night, worried. It was so unlike her not to call if she'd be late. He drove to her favorite spots and scouted around. He looked for her car in all the places he could think of. His calls went straight to voice mail. She never picked up or called back. He grew more frantic as the night faded and the first light announced a new day. By then, Rex was so tired he nodded off while he was driving. Several times he startled himself, jerking awake before almost running into another car. It was pointless to keep going. Surely she'd be home by now, he thought, while driving back to the apartment.

Seeing no signs of her dashed his hopes. He headed inside to catch a quick nap, knowing he wouldn't last through the day otherwise. Rex placed another call to her cell phone and left a frantic, semi-coherent message before crashing on the living room sofa, falling into a deep sleep.

The alarm on his cell phone startled him. He had set the timer to wake him up at 9:30 a.m. Yawning loudly and stretching, he turned it off and got up to make a pot of coffee. While it was brewing, he took a quick shower. Four hours wasn't enough sleep, but the shower refreshed him.

Rex poured a large cup of coffee and sat down to make a list of all the places he had checked already. He tried hard to think of where else Gigi might have gone. It troubled him. This was so unlike her. He placed a call to the office to let them know he wasn't coming in. He liked having the flexibility of being a part-time reporter. As long as he turned his assignments in on time, they left him alone.

Organized and methodical, he crafted a plan including people to call—her friends, family, their mutual acquaintances, anyone who might know where she could be. He called her cell phone again, counting the rings before he left her another message. "Hey, this is Rex, call me *please*. I'm worried. Where are you?"

He went to the kitchen and refilled his cup. Hearing his cell phone jingle with her special ring tone, he rushed back to grab it, spilling hot coffee on his jeans.

"Hello…"

"Oh, Rex…"

"Gigi? Gigi! Where are you?"

"Rex, please come and get me."

"Where? What happened?"

"I… I need your help," she pleaded. "Please hurry. I'm at Hotel Seven."

"On my way," said Rex as he ran out the door, car key in his hands. "I'll be there in about fifteen minutes."

"Okay, I'm inside the lobby." Her phone chirped. "I

need to charge my phone. My battery's going to die at any minute. Got to go."

Rex drove as fast as he dared, mouthing a silent prayer of thanks for the light traffic and hoping he wouldn't get a ticket. He could tell that Gigi wasn't her usual self; she sounded different, maybe even a little scared. That was weird. Rex's impatience matched his speed, his imagination running wild. Where had she been? What happened to her?

Relief was replacing the worry that caused so much angst the night before. His whirling emotions also brought out his feelings for Gigi, and Rex realized they ran deeper than he thought. Well, they were roommates and got along fine. No, cross that out, they were *more* than just roommates. They were best friends. Countless times they helped each other out, and laughed and cried together over the years. They had both dated other people off and on, and in between joked about their nonexistent sex life after their relationships fell through. She'd cried on his shoulder and confided in him. He sought her opinion when he had girlfriend troubles. They had been through so much over the years, staying together as friends while boyfriends or girlfriends came and went. So he knew her pretty well, and he felt sure she knew him.

Rex pulled up in front of Hotel Seven just in time. He didn't see her outside, so he parked and ran into the building to find her. Heart pounding, he panicked when he didn't see her right away. As he scanned the lobby, he spotted her— sitting in a far corner next to the electric outlet she was using to charge her phone.

She jumped up when he rushed across. "You're here!" she shouted, a smile replacing the worried look on her face.

He reached out and wrapped his arms around her, slowly swaying from side to side while hugging her, not willing to let go just yet.

"Gigi, are you all right?" he finally said, pulling back to inspect her.

Gigi nodded. She looked disheveled, her clothes crumpled. She raised her hand, flipping back her hair. "I'm fine. Just a little sore, that's all."

He held her again, rubbing her back gently. "Look, we need to go now. I've got my car parked in front."

She yanked her charger from the wall socket and grabbed her purse. "I could do with a shower and a change of clothing."

On the way out, he maintained protective contact, guiding her by the elbow toward his car. "Maybe I should take you to the hospital, get you checked out first?"

She glanced at him, mumbling, "I don't know... I think I'm okay." She patted her arms, chest, and legs. "I'm all here and in one piece." She added, "I promise I'll let you know if I need to see a doctor."

Rex didn't want to make a fuss. Not here. Not now. They got into his car and he sped straight home.

While Gigi jumped in the shower and freshened up, Rex made breakfast and brewed a fresh pot of coffee. He searched in the refrigerator and found a carton of orange juice, knowing how she liked a little glass of OJ with her breakfast. By the time Gigi finished and got changed, breakfast was on the table.

"Thank you," squealed Gigi as she hugged Rex again. "It smells so good."

Rex was hungry too, he realized, as his own stomach growled. They sat down and ate, not bothering to talk while they gobbled down the eggs and hash potatoes. Satisfied, Rex pushed his plate out of the way and leaned back in his chair.

"So, tell me what happened," he said.

"I don't know how much I remember. It was so odd." Gigi hesitated, searching for the right words. "I think I did something horrible."

Rex waited, knowing she would tell him eventually and it would all come out, piece by piece. That's how they shared and communicated with each other. He let her have as much time as she needed. "I worried about you all night," said Rex. "I kept calling you."

Gigi swallowed, then continued. "I tried to ram my car into a wall. Swerved at the last instant averting a full impact."

"You did... what?"

"I'm sorry, I remember little of what happened after that." She frowned. "I was out... I thought I was, or maybe I dreamt I was laying in a coffin or container." She stared into space trying to recall. "I mean, it was fuzzy. If I'd heard your phone ring, I would have answered." Taking another sip of coffee, Gigi repeated, "You know I would have answered. Maybe I passed out or something like that, and I didn't hear it? That would be a plausible explanation."

"Let's assume that you were unconscious, or out of it after the accident. That may explain why you couldn't remember or didn't hear the phone ring," said Rex. "So what happened when you did wake up? You called me, right?"

"I think so. I heard my phone ring and it woke me up. I must have passed out on the chair in the hotel lobby. When I saw your number on the screen, I called you right back."

"Gosh, does that mean you were out for a long time?"

"Yeah, I suppose."

"So is your car at the hotel?"

"I don't know where my car is."

"Well we should go back over there and look around for it."

Rex drove straight to the hotel parking deck, grabbing a ticket before entering. Crawling at a snail's pace, they looked and checked every vehicle. As they rounded the curve to the exit booth, it became clear that Gigi's car wasn't there.

Finally, Rex suggested widening the search, circling the hotel, combing every side street. This took longer than they thought. They finished by noon, no closer to finding the car than they were in the morning.

# Chapter 8
## ELLEN

Ellen was late when she rushed with her new dress and accessories out of the boutique. She was still pissed at the smooth-talking saleslady encouraging her to try on everything, making suggestions if something didn't work out. Drove her nuts! She wanted to scream and yell, "Don't be so pushy!" She knew the kind. No matter how she looked in the dress, the woman always said, "Ooh, I love this one, it looks great on you." *Ugh.*

Ellen wasn't fooled, knowing full well how she looked. She'd endured cruel taunts for most of her life about her weight, but they got uglier as she got older. Mean, hurtful remarks like, "get that through your fat skull," "fat ass bitch," "you're better off stepping in front of a bus." The bullies from the playground grew up, but they never changed inside.

She'd had to escape from the saleswoman. Worn out and exasperated, Ellen made a quick selection—a stylish dress catching her attention, but one she knew was too small—

just to get rid of the woman. It wasn't an easy way out—an expensive choice, definitely hard on her pocketbook.

The rush-hour traffic was horrendous. Cars inched along, creeping and crawling. Ellen had no patience, tapping her fingers on the wheel as she looked around, waiting for the light to change. To her left was another shopping strip. A sign caught her eye. Eve's Alterations. On impulse, she flicked her turn signal, waving to the man driving his truck toward her in the opposite lane to catch his attention. She flashed her cutest smile. He smiled back and stopped, letting her make the turn.

Men liked Ellen if all they could see was her pretty face.

Ellen parked, grabbing the bag with her new dress. Clutching the undersized garment, she had to admit how much she liked it despite it being the wrong size, so much so that she'd fantasized wearing it and showing off at her cousin's wedding. Ever since she got the invitation in the mail, she was obsessed with the thought of going back home looking good, *damn good*. The hometown girl is not looking frumpy. She'd show up at the wedding and dazzle everyone. Okay, that was just wishful thinking. She reluctantly dropped the dress back in the shopping bag. Maybe, if this seamstress was worth her salt, she could look stunning.

A bell announced her entrance as Ellen opened the door.

"Hello. Anyone here?" said Ellen, peering inside. It was a plain room with a counter, a cash register, and a curtained changing room.

"Wait a minute, be out soon," a female voice called from the back.

"Okay," Ellen shouted. Waiting, she glanced around and

saw two displays on the wall—the business license and another cheap frame with a mounted dollar bill. It was considered good luck to save the first dollar bill earned, rather than spend it. No other decorations graced the walls. It was what she expected. Alterations was what she came here for, not some fancy interior decorating.

The curtain was pulled aside, and a diminutive, dark-haired woman appeared.

"Hello," she said with a smile. "You come here."

"Hi, I'm Ellen. You are Eve?"

"Eve."

Ellen held up her new dress, flaunting it. The vivid deep blue, the V-neck, the hand-beaded lace bodice, and the three-quarter length sleeves were dazzling.

The seamstress gestured Ellen closer, then made a circle with her finger. "Turn around please." She held up the dress to Ellen's back, measuring with her well-trained eyes. It didn't take her more than a second to realize the dress was about two to three sizes smaller. She stared at Ellen and said, "You *like* this dress?"

"Oh *yes*, very much," Ellen said, nodding emphatically. "I'm planning to wear it to a wedding." Ellen had lost thirty-five pounds already, coming down three dress sizes. But still at one fifty-five, she had a ways to go. Her goal of losing another thirty pounds before the wedding now appeared hopeless, along with fitting into this gorgeous size six dress.

The seamstress handed the dress back to Ellen. "Okay, I know what you need." She opened a drawer behind the counter, picking up a brochure to show Ellen.

"What's this?" Ellen asked.

"This is for a special lady like you," Eve said.

"Tell me what it is."

"You look…" Eve said, handing her the brochure.

Curious, Ellen's eyes scanned the contents.

"This brochure, it's not about the sewing alterations," said Ellen. "It says, 'Instant body slimming for the look you desire.'" Her eyes skimmed to the price column, but all it said was MARKET PRICE. It looked like a Chinese restaurant menu. "How much is the market price?"

"Which one you want? See here," said Eve as she pointed to the three choices. "Option A, Size 6, in the middle Option B, Size 8, and on the right Option C, Size 10. You pick."

"I don't understand. I thought 'alterations' is for the dress—or a blouse, pants, suit…" She paused.

"No alteration dress, alteration your body to fit dress." Eve pulled out a tablet. "Let me show you." She scrolled through a series of photos labeled "Before" and "After"— each having a silhouette of a body next to the dress. The only thing that changed from "Before" to "After" was the size of the person.

Ellen felt a chill run up her back as she realized what Eve was showing her. The photos showed the size of the *person* had been altered—not the dress.

"How do you get smaller to fit into the dress?" Ellen was interested, although perplexed at the same time.

Eve said, "No operation." She scrolled to the page with the three options. "You pick one."

Curious to see where this was going, Ellen played along, entering the size of her new dress. Option A appeared with the text, "Are you sure you want Option A, Size 6?"

Ellen touched the YES button. Then, the page displayed an appointment time for that evening with an address.

Eve went to the back room and returned with a printed sheet for Ellen. "All done."

"Do I pay you now?"

"No pay me. When you go to appointment."

Ellen looked at the slip. The date and time was tonight at 8:00 p.m. That left just enough time to get a quick bite at the drive-through. She grabbed her dress, hurrying out.

# Chapter 9
## ELLEN

Ellen got to the appointment location early. Relaxing in her car seat, she thought about the whole day—a whirlwind, running from meeting to meeting, eating on the run, fighting the traffic. Closing her eyes, she went over what Eve said. Ellen could tell that Eve, the seamstress, either didn't know the answers or wasn't able to explain to her satisfaction what the options entailed. She would ask her questions and find out tonight.

The location on the sheet Eve gave her was at the corner of two streets. It didn't have an exact street number or name of the business. Ellen scanned the building in sight. It was strange. Absorbed in studying the map on her cell phone, she didn't see or hear the man until he tapped on her car window, startling her.

"Are you Ellen?"

"Who… are you? How did you know?"

"You can get out of your car and follow me," he said, not bothering to answer her questions.

"I'm here for my appointment, but I don't know where to go."

"Just follow me. I'm here to take you there."

She grabbed the dress and her appointment slip. Leaving her car parked by the side of the street, she locked it and followed the man to the nondescript office building at the corner.

He pointed inside, leaving as she entered the lobby. On the wall before the elevators, Ellen saw the directory of businesses. Reading through the names, she ruled out, by a process of elimination, businesses that obviously didn't fit. That narrowed it down to two possibilities.

She typed both of those office numbers in her cell phone notes and rode the elevator to the first one on the second floor. Ellen knocked on the office door and waited. No one came to the door or answered. She knocked again. Nothing. So she went back in the elevator and pushed the fourth floor button. She found Room 408 at the end of the hallway. At first knock, a young man opened the door and welcomed her. "Hello."

"Hi, I'm Ellen. My appointment is at 8:00 p.m."

"Yes, we're expecting you. I'm Daman. Please come in and have a seat in this room. The doctor will be with you in a minute."

Ellen walked in, surprised at the pleasant surroundings. Fresh white paint covered the walls. Together with the minimalist white furniture and the stylish tiny reception desk, it conveyed a crisp, clean, no-nonsense atmosphere.

"Can you tell me about the procedure?"

29

"The doctor will explain it to you."

"It's not an operation is it?" she asked with concern, letting him know she was not up to something like that. "I hate surgeries; they scare me."

He reassured her, speaking in a cheerful way. "No ma'am, we don't do that here. You'll be out of here soon." He paused and added, "And looking great."

"Oh," she said as the doctor stepped into the room to greet her.

"Good evening, you must be Ellen. I'm Dr. Kite."

She extended her hand. "Hi, yes, I'm Ellen Fulbright. Nice to meet you, Doctor."

"Come with me. We'll sit down and talk first." She followed him down the hall to his office, and he waved for her to sit. "I know you have questions. Now, what would you like to know?"

Ellen pursed her lips. "I selected Option A on the menu for Size 6 dress." She pulled out her dress for him to see, shaking it for emphasis. "How do you get me to fit into this dress?"

He was ready for her. "You selected Option A. When you walk out of here tonight, you'll be wearing that dress."

"But how is that possible? I *don't* want anyone to operate on me."

"There's no surgery. I assure you. It will be a gentle and quick, and you will not feel any pain." He paused, reaching on his desk for a pen—well, something that looked like a pen. "See this?"

She nodded, wondering why he was holding it.

"Inside is a mini-syringe. Injection is quick and painless—just a small pinch, hardly more than a mosquito bite." Kite touched the pen on his arm to show her.

"What are you injecting?"

"I will insert a tiny microchip inside your body. It will adjust your metabolism to what you eat."

"How does your chip work?"

"It works on a cellular level, regulating the mitochondria. Your chip increases the rate of fat metabolism."

"You mean I can still eat whatever I want, and how much I want?"

"Not exactly. It will have to work harder if you eat more. So I suggest eating smaller portions at more frequent intervals. Can you do that?"

"I've been on a diet and lost thirty-five pounds, cutting out a lot of carbs and eating less."

"So you want to lose more weight?"

"Well I need help now. I've been struggling to get the last thirty pounds off and *nothing* I do seems to make a difference."

"We'll give a boost to blast the fat cells tonight that'll take about twenty minutes. That will drop you down to the size you selected immediately. Then the procedure to inject the microchip takes a few seconds. But remember, to maintain your size six, you must also change your eating habits."

"What happens if I don't... if I forget?"

"We've programmed a reminder, adjusted to the level of overconsumption and pain threshold."

"Pain? What kind of pain?" Ellen asked, shifting in her seat.

"It's a mild reminder at first, like a tiny prick." He

quickly added, "But if it's too much, we can tweak it."

"I… I'm not sure I like that." She hesitated.

"The pain reminder?"

"Yeah."

"Hmm," he said, sighing. "On second thought, no—instead I'm going to use the new second-generation, upgraded chip I just got. It has a mind control element to ensure you'll change your behavior."

"Mind control?"

"Yes, the new chips have this, an enhancement over the older chip that uses pain to control behavior."

"So, uh, I won't get a pain reminder?"

"Right. I just received this new shipment. There's one with the blue label for overweight clients. You'll get that one."

"That sounds too good to be true."

"It's the best I can offer you."

"Will I look different tonight after this procedure?"

"You'll be thinner, just like in the photos you've seen. And you'll fit into your size six dress."

"How safe is this new procedure?"

"It's safe. We've had no problems. You can think about it and call me later if you have more questions."

She stared at him intently. "It really works *and* it's safe?"

"Yes." He pushed back his chair to stand. "Do you want to think it over, or shall we do it tonight?"

"One more question. If I change my mind, can you remove this chip?"

"At any time, if you request it. And I'll give you this one-time offer of a free trial period."

"Okay, then I'm ready," said Ellen, smiling as she stood up.

Ellen followed Kite down the hall to another white room lit with soft lights. A white pod was in the middle of the room. A table stood next to it with a tray on top. A pen lay on the tray next to a strip of alcohol pads and gauze.

"Please lie down in the pod. You can take your clothes off and leave your underwear on, then drape this sheet over yourself. I'll give you a few minutes and come back."

After he left, Ellen inspected the pod. It looked elegantly designed, a white, clamshell-like structure that appeared translucent. Ellen put her dress over the chair and took off her clothes down to her lace bra and panties before climbing a white two-step stool into the pod. She smoothed the cloth over her, scooping her long hair to one side and closing her eyes. She sensed his presence a moment before he spoke.

"Ellen, I want you to relax and keep your eyes closed. Visualize your new look, your new size. I will close the lid of the pod, but you will still be able to hear me."

He kept talking for a few minutes in a soothing voice. She drifted in and out of wakefulness, waiting for the procedure and thinking, *when will this happen?* She tried to calm her unease and assure herself that this wasn't an operation. Ellen finally relaxed and fell asleep. At some point, the clamshell opened and she thought she felt a slight pinch on her arm.

"You may get up whenever you are ready."

Ellen opened her eyes. The doctor was gone. *What? Is it done already?*

She looked around, then touched herself with the tips of her fingers—exploring. She slowly sat up, and then swung her leg out to climb out of the clamshell, placing her foot on the step stool first.

Someone had taken her dress and hung it on a hanger. Slipping the dress over her head, Ellen felt it glide over her body. She knew. *Without a doubt.*

The doctor and Daman greeted her when she rushed to the door and opened it. The looks on their faces said it all, without a single word exchanged. Ellen was ecstatic. She twirled around, showing off how she looked from every angle, adding a dance step or two as a bonus.

The younger guy grinned from ear to ear. Adjusting the standing mirror to provide a better view, he said, "Here, have a look."

# Chapter 10

## GIGI

Rex's first idea should have been to call the wreckers or impound lots. Without wasting more time, they went back home. While he searched on the Internet, Gigi went to lie down. He checked in on Gigi as she slept. He didn't disturb her; letting her sleep was the best thing for her right now. He left a note, tacking the yellow sticky on her night table where she would be sure to see it when she woke up. The note told her where he would be—at the office—and to call him when she awoke.

Rex got out his keys and left. It bugged him he couldn't do more than he did. She had been through a lot. Yet, he wondered if there was more that she hadn't yet shared with him. Sometimes she held back, not because she wasn't upfront with him, but because she didn't want him to worry about her. What good would that do? One of them had to be the sane one at all times. He respected that. She was right about most things. It wasn't as if he would stop worrying, but he knew talking helped to take a load off her mind. He was that person, that confidant, that best friend.

Rex stepped off the elevator and walked through the press offices to his cubicle. He had another, ulterior motive for coming in today. Scrolling through his contact list, he found his friend Steve, who was a consultant and sometimes a private investigator after his retirement from the force. He dialed his number.

"Hi buddy, Rex."

"Oh, hey," said Steve, genuinely glad to hear from him. "How've you been?"

"Doing good. And you?"

"Can't say I have any complaints." He paused. "How's Gigi?"

Rex gave Steve a rundown of what had happened to Gigi. He wanted Steve's perspective. Maybe he was missing something. Not willing to leave it at that, he told Steve everything. Steve was superb at what he did. And if anyone could help, he could.

"I'm just in a rut, Steve," confessed Rex, running his fingers through his hair. "Something doesn't seem right, and Gigi can't remember what happened. It's like someone or something wiped her memory clean for those hours."

"I know you're worried, Rex. Let me see what I can find out."

Rex could hear Steve clicking on the computer while they talked.

"Thanks, Steve. I'm grateful for anything you can do to help."

"I'm looking at reports of cars or accidents. Do you have the vehicle information and the tag number of Gigi's car?"

"Yes, it's an old car." Rex read out the tag number and gave Steve the year, make, model, and color. He could hear more clicking.

"Ah… here," said Steve. "I found a report of an abandoned car near the Highway 15 underpass. The description matches Gigi's car." He continued after a brief pause. "You'd better get there fast. They'll be taking her car to impound."

"I'll go get Gigi. Thanks, man."

# Chapter 11
## ELLEN

Ellen stood naked in front of the floor-length mirror in her bedroom. Her eyes scrutinized every part of her body from her head to her toes. She turned around, craning her neck over her shoulder. She sauntered back and forth in front of the mirror, admiring her perfect body—the proportionate curves, perky round breasts, smooth flat stomach, long tapering legs, and firm butt. She looked better than she ever had. *Way* better. She smiled as she strutted confidently, head held high.

Her cousin's upcoming wedding increased the pressure on her. Ellen had struggled with her weight for years and uled just about every diet and exercise program. Her tummy area was the worst. She hadn't been able to get rid of the fat there. Her hips, butt, and outer thighs padded fat faster than she could get rid of it.

Every choice of clothing was calculated to camouflage her problems. The dress sizes increased with the years. It became hopeless, affecting other aspects of her life. It wasn't just her weight that dragged down her confidence, but also the depressing thought of the not-too-distant future, in a few years, when she would turn forty.

She was tired of it all. She didn't know what to do anymore. Nothing she did ever worked for long. Sure, she had lost weight with some diets, but gained it all back eventually. She got to the point where she was disgusted whenever she looked in the mirror—each time she'd spent more money and chased after a new fad diet.

Ellen had reached the point of desperation when she met Kite. She had to do something—something that she couldn't achieve herself, and it had to be something that worked fast, in time for the wedding. Kite promised that and delivered—he got rid of that fat immediately and gave Ellen a new body—a total body transformation. She absolutely loved it.

She left the doctor's office elated. He told her it was time phased. This was a trial run at no cost. If she wanted to keep going, she would need to pay. It was expensive, but in the long run, cheaper than an operation. Kite gave her a stern reminder about the expiration date and time, which turned out to be six days after the Saturday wedding at 8:30 p.m. If she didn't pay by then, the time would expire on the microchip. The doctor emphasized the importance of the deadline. If she waited past the deadline, it would be too late, and the door on that offer would shut forever.

# Chapter 12

## GIGI

"Gigi," whispered Rex as he shook her shoulders gently. "Wake up, they found your car." He waited, then shook her again, more firmly this time. He spoke with more urgency. "Get up now."

She stirred and moved her body ever so slightly. "What?" she mumbled.

"Gigi, they found your car. Get up. We need to go *now.*"

Her eyes popped open. "My car? Where is my car?"

"It's near the Highway 15 underpass."

Gigi jumped out of bed, awake now. She yelled, "Give me a minute, I'll be right out."

"I'll be waiting in the car," said Rex, rushing out the door.

Rex drove as fast as he dared to the Highway 15 underpass. He knew the place, having passed through there many times. As they approached, it was evident the guy from the wrecker service was already there getting ready to tow her car.

40

"*Wait*, please wait a minute," shouted Rex as he and Gigi ran toward him.

The guy looked up as he hopped on the bed of the truck, checking the tow straps and fiddling with the tow chains. "Is that your car?"

"Yes. We'd like to take a quick look. Can you please wait?" pleaded Rex, the urgency in his voice matching his expression.

"You got about a minute until I get this chain untangled."

They approached the car, which was parked at an angle on the grassy strip area next to the highway. From the looks of the tire marks and tracks on the grass, the car had swerved at the last minute to avoid running into the concrete wall, so the force of the hit was not full frontal, but it had sheared off the side rearview mirror and damaged the corner and the side of the car where it scraped the underpass wall. A few pieces of paper lay scattered on the grass on the driver side, where they had blown out of the half rolled-down window. It was very fortunate that Gigi didn't run straight into the wall. The car could have exploded in flames, engulfing and destroying the vehicle with her inside.

"Do you think it's totaled?" blurted Rex, even though he knew the answer.

The wrecker guy gave a sympathetic nod, then finished hooking up the chains and pulling the car onto his flatbed. Before he left, he gave Rex a card. "Call this number."

"Thanks, man."

Rex looked over at Gigi. She had been silent as she surveyed the accident scene. He hoped she wasn't traumatized. Survivor shock, PTSD, emotional trauma—those could stay with you long afterwards. He remembered his first car, a tiny little Volks. Oh, how he enjoyed driving that thing until someone rear-ended him one day. *Pow!* The moment of impact, his body jerking, his head thrown back and forth. He had been shaken and couldn't stop trembling. That memory still lingered on.

This incident happened in an odd place. What was Gigi doing there? Why did she pick this location? The underpass was off the beaten path and not in a well-traveled territory.

Rex watched the tow truck pull away and waited until the dust settled before approaching Gigi, who was still sitting on the grass. He scooted next to her. They sat for a while, staring in silence at the empty spot where her car had been. Finally, he leaned forward to whisper in her ear. "You feeling okay?"

"Yeah, but not about the accident. I mean, it *was* an accident, right? It had to be." She looked confused, searching for answers. "I don't remember what I was doing here or why I drove this way. I don't know why I'd be running into the wall or why I didn't." She gestured wildly, pointing to the concrete barrier, then shuddered.

"Just calm down, Do you remember anything? Anything at all? Try to go back over the steps if you can."

"I tried… can't…" She sighed.

"Were you swerving to avoid hitting someone? A dog or a critter… like a squirrel?"

"I don't remember… why would I ram it?"

"Well, you're lucky you didn't. Else I wouldn't be sitting here talking to you."

Gigi twisted her face, feeling the tears welling up. Then she released her pent-up emotions, holding nothing back. He wrapped his arms around her, comforting her, feeling the weight of her head resting on his shoulder as she cried, her tears soaking the cotton of his shirt.

# Chapter 13

## DR. KITE

Kite picked up the phone. "Okay, bring her here. I'll be ready." He had been waiting for this call. When it finally happened, he was pleased. Ever since the night he had dinner with Lilly Cooper, he hadn't been able to get her off his mind. He was interested in her, and thought she might be interested in him too, although she gave no obvious signs of encouragement for anything else in the future. From what he observed, she seemed lonely, but not desperate. Maybe he was in the right place at the right time. He was curious and excited, wondering what Lilly was really like. She appeared reserved and polite. Was it just a thin veneer of aloofness or was she cold deep down, all the way to her heart?

Emboldened to impress her, throwing caution to the wind this time, he'd offered her his second-generation microchip—a new body and mind, a new chance in life. He made it clear she must be discreet and gave her his business card so she could call if she ever needed him.

He arranged for Gary, a cab driver that he often used, to

be on the lookout for her after that night at the restaurant. Gary watched Lilly and followed her for a couple of days to get an idea of her itinerary, routines, and travel patterns. Kite toyed with the idea of casually bumping into Lilly, but he didn't. He believed everything happened for a reason. And so he waited.

When she finally called, Kite told her he would send a taxi to pick her up and bring her to him. Rubbing the palms of his hands together in anticipation, he was overcome with excitement and joy. Fortunately, he had a new upgraded mind control microchip left from the last shipment on Monday for Lilly, the one with the purple label that reversed aging on a cellular level. He had already used the other two—injecting Gigi with the red-labeled microchip that cured her illness and Ellen with the blue-labeled one that controlled her weight. Today was Lilly's lucky day.

The taxi pulled up to the building. Gary glanced at the back seat, checking on his passenger. The doctor would be pleased. Gary knew how much he trusted him, and he was moving up the ranks fast. He put on his best smile and opened the car door for Lilly. She barely glanced at him, focusing her attention on the doctor instead.

Kite rushed to greet Lilly, taking her by the arm and nodding his thanks to Gary before escorting her inside his new office with its fresh white paint and hygienic, sterile-looking rooms. He opened this second location to garner new clients, the paying kind. The sordid warehouse had served its purpose. It would be closing soon with the impending success of the second- generation microchip.

As Lilly lay on the table, the doctor took his time, pulling over his tray and explaining the procedure. The injection pen had been loaded up with the upgraded mind control chip Lilly demanded once he explained it could give her body the youth she'd lost and drive out the bitterness that lingered after the divorce, freeing her from the past and releasing her to start a new life. The timing was perfect. In his eagerness to give her what she needed, what she insisted on getting now, he also skipped the trial period with an end date like the one he'd programmed into Ellen's chip.

# Chapter 14

## ELLEN

Ellen pranced around, reluctant to take off her new dress. The longer she wore it, the happier she felt. She bent to touch her toes. No problem. She hadn't been able to do that for ages. She couldn't wait to buy new clothes—nothing in her closet fit now. She called her mom, managing a quick winded, "Hi, Mom."

"Hey Elly, I'm so glad you called."

"Yeah, Mom." At first, her Mom was the only one who called her Elly and got away with it. When the kids found out, they teased her mercilessly at school. "Elly the hilly… has a big belly." The taunts were hurtful and she never forgot them. She begged her Mom to stop calling her Elly. *Please mom, please stop!* But she never did. She was stuck on calling her Elly and never changed it. "Hey, you've got my room ready for next week? You know I'm coming home for the wedding."

"Oh hon, we thought you'd be coming. But your cousin said she mailed you the wedding invitation three weeks ago."

She paused. "Have you sent back your RSVP?"

"Sorry, Mom, I forgot. I'll send it tomorrow."

"I told her you were busy and to please save you a place in case you forgot to mail it." She sighed, irritated at her flighty daughter. "You know, if it wasn't for your cousin, you wouldn't be getting a seat at the reception dinner."

"Err, well… thanks, Mom."

"Be sure to get a nice—I mean, a *very* nice gift for your cousin."

"Okay, I will. See you next weekend."

Ending the call, Ellen picked up her slim new pink pen and added *get a very nice gift* to her to-do list before the wedding. She didn't want to tell her Mom yet about her new look. The thought of surprising her in person was worth the wait.

# Chapter 15
## GIGI

Something was bugging Steve after the call with Rex. He was old enough to be his father, but they were good friends. Steve had envied Rex the first time he met Gigi. She was in her early twenties, and he couldn't believe how gorgeous and nice she was. Surely they were dating? But Rex assured him they were only roommates and were seeing other people.

Steve could tell something was worrying Rex the moment he spoke. The thing that happened to Gigi was weird, out of the blue and so out of character.

After Rex told him where Gigi was found, he had gone to the hotel and talked the staff into letting him see the security camera tapes. Sure enough, she appeared on them. He had rewound it back to the time shortly before she called Rex. The tapes showed her in the hotel lobby at that time. It was just as Rex said, even the details. What puzzled him was the camera footage before she got there. It was angled, not facing the elevator, so there wasn't a good shot of the doors opening when Gigi came into the lobby. He caught a

blur of three people walking across the room, two men with
Gigi in the middle. He would have to figure out some other
way to find out who brought her in the hotel.

# Chapter 16
## DR. KITE

Kite made a few notes. Right now things were going well. The hiccup had been Gigi. He toyed over the possibilities. Sometimes the modern microchips malfunctioned, but that was so rare, and it hadn't been a problem yet. Or the person may have reacted to it for some other reason. He had gotten a new batch of upgraded microchips a few days ago, the ones with the mind control, and they came in three tubes that were color labeled—red, blue, and purple. For Gigi, he'd picked red, the same color as the original microchip that cured her tinnitus.

Since the early days, Kite used loners or vagrants who wouldn't be easily traced or missed by family as test subjects. In his desperation to succeed, he experimented on involuntary human subjects, violating the ethics of human experimentation.

Obsessed, he had devoured every piece of scientific literature, taking special interest in another company that showed early promise in the research of implantable

JANE SUEN

microchips. But after unacceptable risks and side effects came to light, that company abandoned its research. Kite persisted, his curiosity and intellect challenged. Years of meticulous experiments bore no fruit until, one day, pure luck brought a chance discovery. He made arrangements with an offshore laboratory to make the chips. This led to the first generation of implantable microchips that altered physical aspects.

He had developed three prototypes distinguished by red, blue, and purple labels—one to cure illnesses and heal injuries, one to re-sculpture and lose fat, and one to rejuvenate and reverse the aging process. The second-generation of microchips took it a step further, incorporating advanced technology to alter the mind. This phase of the project was the most challenging. He was at the point of giving up when he came across the renegade microchip. Instead of tossing it, he studied it to figure out how the renegade took over the person's mind.

This upgraded chip was to be an improvement over the first, by adding mind control in sync with the body's changes to fortify the mind-body connection. If this worked, his next improved model would be a nanochip, incredibly tiny yet powerful, and specifically programmed to target cells with unparalleled speed and precision. He savored the thought of releasing an army of nanobots, not only to seek and kill cells, but also to replace and replicate—even itself.

# Chapter 17

## LILLY

The divorce left its mark on Lilly, turning her into a bitter and angry woman. She had devoted her whole life to Frank, helping him build his business. She didn't have any kids— Frank was absolutely firm that he didn't want any. Every time she thought of Frank, her fingers inevitably flexed into a claw-like grasp. She would have dug out Frank's eyes if she could. How dare he take the best years of her life and all she offered, then get rid of her after she helped him achieve his goals? He couldn't have done any of it without her.

The night she was at the restaurant, Lilly was contemplating her fate. She wanted revenge. Frank was stingy with her in the divorce, and she had to fight for every penny. Frank wasn't going to give it to her otherwise. She clung to the bitterness, fueling her regret at the years wasted on that man.

Now that she was divorced, even her freedom failed to provide solace. No longer would she have to spend hours worrying about Frank's business. Funny, that should have been a clue… it was always *Frank's*, never Frank *and* Lilly's. He never referred to it that way when he talked, and her name wasn't on the website, the business card, or anywhere else. Now she understood why he acted that way—he wanted to keep it all to himself. That should have been a warning sign. She had asked him often, but he so effortlessly brushed away her requests with a noncommittal remark.

If only she hadn't been so trusting, if she hadn't been so focused on the business, she might have noticed that he was dallying with that fool girl, his office assistant. He was still cautious before the divorce—Lilly guessed he didn't want to lose it all to her. Afterward, she heard he married that girl and they had a baby. Imagine that, Frank who *never* wanted kids. Instead, she was bringing him another mouth to feed. Lilly shook her head.

At the restaurant, Lilly had been in a foul mood before Kite arrived. She stewed as she settled in and ordered dinner. But as she sipped the wine and tasted the fine food, her frosty exterior gradually warmed as the craving and emptiness in her stomach eased. She started to feel better.

Lilly had just ordered coffee and dessert when the hostess, Sally, arrived at her table with Kite in tow. Sally's usual upbeat manner turned fluctered when she saw Lilly.

"Sally, it's okay," said Lilly softly, so only Sally could hear. "It's not a big deal. There's room for two at this table. I don't bite."

Truth be told, Kite wasn't bad company. The man liked to talk, and she let him. Oh, how he went on and on. But it was pleasant. She made a slight effort to engage in small talk.

But she didn't expect too much. After all, they were just sharing a table. If things had turned sour, she was prepared to make an excuse and dash out, taking the dessert to go.

Luckily that didn't happen. She let Kite babble on and on. He apparently thought she was enjoying the conversation.

But she was tuning him out a little at a time. One had to be careful with this charade. You could nod every once in a while to give the impression that you've heard and understand what your table companion was saying. But if you nodded at an inappropriate time, or affirmed something that was said but you had no clue to what it was, you could get into trouble. And then, there's the yawn. That had worked too. She could throw her head back, for effect, and give a long slow yawn, also for effect. Add a few shoulder shrugs and then gestures to gather her things to go while stifling another yawn, then muttering, "I really must go. It's past my bedtime." This trick usually generated jokes from the unsuspecting other party about bedtime for a full-grown woman. Nothing like leaving the other party laughing.

# Chapter 18

## GIGI

The worst thing was the waiting.

Gigi was thankful to have Rex by her side. It made the whole ordeal bearable. If he hadn't made that call to Steve, they wouldn't have found her car before it was towed away. She knew how lucky she was to have survived—with not even a scrape or broken bone in her body. She felt like the luckiest girl alive, grateful to God she hadn't been seriously injured, paralyzed, or worse. Had she driven on the road and swerved toward the wall because of a deer or a squirrel, or something else? Had she fallen asleep and woken up at the last minute in time to avert a head-on crash? Or—the unthinkable—had she *wanted* to run straight into the wall? She might never know if she couldn't remember the accident, but she did realize she had a second chance in life.

The night before the accident, in her dreams, she had almost crossed over to the other side and was hanging by a rope over the precipice. Then she heard someone calling her, "Gigi, wake up!" She must have cried out in her sleep in her fear of falling over the edge.

When she opened her eyes, Rex was leaning over her bed, the loose tendrils of his shoulder-length hair tickling her face as he shook her.

"You're having some badass nightmare." His face had looked funny, scrunched with concern and fear.

"Yeah."

"Those nightmares. Are they new?"

"Yes, they started recently," said Gigi, and she went on to describe the terrifying new dreams that started a few nights ago at the time the new mind control chip was implanted. Her explanation stopped here—she never told Rex about her treatment by Kite and the chip. He didn't know.

"No wonder you screamed."

"I was scared shitless, it seemed so real." Gigi laughed nervously. "I could see it, my breath frosting in the cold. I could feel it, the wind blowing, swaying me as I held on to the rope over the precipice... the dark void below." She gulped. "It felt so real—so frightening. I thought I'd die right then and there."

Rex had comforted her that night in the best way he could. Keeping his voice low, soothing, and calming, he held her in his arms as he felt her muscles gradually relax, letting go of the tension. She had experienced extreme fear, so real and inescapable. Her body had been in a fight-or-flight mode and frozen. If it had gotten any worse, he worried that she'd have a heart attack. They say you can die of fright, and he believed there was truth to that.

"There, there," said Rex. "Shh… shh." He gently rocked her back and forth. Her fearful state reminded him of a frightened rabbit with its eyes fixated in terror, held in the headlights of an oncoming car. Frozen in mid-stride, unable to move, unable to save itself from the crushing weight of the car as it rushed closer, bringing death.

# Chapter 19

## ELLEN

The plane taxied down to the end of the runway, next in line to go. The flaps on the wings made a whirring sound as they opened. Ellen re-checked her seat belt. She chewed her gum furiously, sitting back in her seat with her eyes closed, bracing as the engine revved and the plane prepared to take off.

Airborne, she heard the mechanical sounds of the wheels retracting and the wing flaps closing back up as the plane gained attitude, finally reaching cruising speed. In a few hours, she would be back at the family home and in her old bedroom. She focused on that. She took a deep breath, keeping her eyes shut, and settled in for the trip.

"What would you like to drink, sir?" asked the flight attendant, speaking to the guy in the aisle seat. Ellen was barely awake when she heard this. She briefly considered forgoing the drink and pretzels to keep on dozing. She had a few seconds to decide before the man next to her would be served and the cart would start moving down the aisle. If she kept her eyes closed, they wouldn't disturb her.

Hearing the drop of ice cubes in the cup, the fizz of the can opening, and the rattling of cubes as the guy drank, Ellen sat up. The stewardess smiled and asked the same question. "What would you like to drink?"

"I'll have tonic water, please," said Ellen as she pulled the tray table down.

"Pretzel?"

"Yes, please."

The stewardess handed her a pack before pushing the cart along.

Ellen looked over the pretzel package, but couldn't find the little tear mark. "Cheap shit," she muttered under her breath. "Cheap fucking shit."

"May I give you a hand?" said the guy sitting next to her, who had been watching all this with a bemused look.

*Oh God no, he's heard me cursing.* Slipping an embarrassed glance at the smartly dressed man, Ellen couldn't help blushing and thinking, *What a cute guy.* "Sure, give it a try if you like," said Ellen as she handed it to him with a coy smile. No harm in trying to repair the damage.

He didn't bother looking for the notches, just gripped the packet with both hands and tore it open with a practiced smooth motion. "Here," he said with a grin. "Enjoy your pretzels."

"I sure lucked out sitting next to Mr. Superman," said Ellen. Remembering her manners, she said, "Okay, let's start over. Hi, I'm Ellen."

"I'm Brad," he said. "Nice to meet you."

"You have a way with pretzels, you know."

"And you have a way with men."

"Are you hitting on me?"

"Only if you say so."

She laughed. "Okay, let's start over *again*. I'm Ellen, and I am traveling to Woodville to attend my cousin's wedding."

"Hi, I'm Brad, and I have a stopover at Woodville before catching a plane to Denver for a business meeting."

"What line of work are you in?"

"Investment, real estate, and a bit of import-export."

"Business good these days?"

"Yes, right now real estate markets are flooded with foreign investors coming here to buy property. Real estate is a safer bet."

"You travel a lot?"

"A little too much sometimes. My home is here. I've got a place on the north side."

"I live here too. I have an apartment in the city. Close to everything."

"You like what you do?"

"Most days. You know it's crazy sometimes. I'm good at what I do. I'm an administrative assistant."

"We all have to make a living somehow," said Brad. "Unless you're independently wealthy or you win the lottery."

Ellen laughed. Sweet dreams. At first look, Brad seemed really young, but she guessed he was a little bit older, maybe in his early thirties. Very well-groomed, clean-shaven, a nice crew cut, and an aftershave with a subtle scent of virile masculinity.

She wanted to ask Brad outright what he used as aftershave, but decided she'd steer the conversation elsewhere first. "You know, my dad was an aftershave guy, and he used the same brand for over thirty years."

Brad lifted an eyebrow, brown eyes curious.

"He refused to try a different brand, even when we bought him other ones for his birthday presents," said Ellen. "Do you think men are more loyal or less adventurous?"

"You're asking about aftershave or men in general?"

"Hmm… aftershave, but yeah."

"I personally think men are mostly creatures of habit. My dad was the same way, he used the same aftershave for years too," said Brad with a twinkle in his eyes. "I used to try his when I was a kid. I'd climb up on the bathroom counter top to reach the cabinet door to get it. He always kept it in the same place too." He paused, shaking his head, then continued. "Once when I grabbed that blue bottle, it slipped out of my tiny hands, smashing on the floor. I was mortified. My mind whipped through all kinds of scenarios of what my dad would do to punish me."

"Uh oh, then what happened? Did he beat you?"

Reflecting for a moment, Brad said, "As luck would have it, my mom was in the bedroom when it happened. She heard the bottle shatter, and me bawling my eyes out. She rushed over and held me until my crying stopped, then helped clean it up. We headed over to the nearest store and got another one. My dad never found out about it."

"Your mom spared you from his punishment."

"Yup, and I learned my lesson," said Brad, a bit of pride

sneaking into his voice. "And I paid my mom back out of my paper boy earnings."

"I like your mom," said Ellen with a nod.

The rest of the flight went too quickly, as they chatted and laughed the rest of the way. After the plane landed, they parted ways, but not before they had exchanged phone numbers and made plans for dinner in a week, when they were both back home.

# Chapter 20
## LILLY

"Watch your step, ma'am," said Gary, holding the umbrella over Lilly's head as she stepped out of the cab. Overhead, the raindrops spattered big clumpy drops and the thunder roared. Gary had parked the taxi close to the sidewalk in front of her home so he could walk her up the steps to the front door of her brick townhouse. She told him she hated days like this and didn't have an umbrella.

Gary loved the rain, whether watching from inside the house or being outside in it. He didn't mind getting wet at all. As a child, he used to play a game, counting the seconds between the lightning flash and thunder clap, and making a big dip of his hands, like a conductor with his baton, when he timed the clap of thunder just right. He played it so many times it became his favorite pastime when it rained.

Today the gods were angry and wouldn't let up. When the clouds grew dark and pulled the curtain over the sky, he knew it'd be a fierce storm, like the weatherman predicted. Not a quick summer storm that blew over almost as soon as it started. This one was loud, angry, demanding, and full of raging sparks and forceful energy. The rain pelted mercilessly, not slowing down. The wind added its chorus to the thunder and blew gusts that toppled signs, downed trees, and lifted anything it could move or carry in its path.

Gary guided Lilly across the pavement and up the steps of her townhouse, shielding her with his body and deflecting the rain with the umbrella. When the lightning flashed, Gary was so intent on counting the seconds until the thunder that he took his eyes off Lilly for a moment. As the gods would have it, it was perfectly timed so that a mighty gust of wind inverted the umbrella and almost sent it flying out of his grip. Instantly, a torrent of rain came down hard on Lilly's head, catching her by surprise as it pelted water on her face and shoulders. The metal ribs of the umbrella flapped helplessly, slapping more water on her.

In a flash, she turned around to face Gary, her features contorted, ugly and demonic. Growling, Lilly uttered a deep, guttural sound—chilling and feral.

Before Gary could react, Lilly savagely pushed him. He teetered on the edge of the step, trying to catch his balance, desperately gripping the umbrella and impervious to the rain that soaked his clothes. At that moment in time, in an instant that seemed like an eternity, he looked desperately into Lilly's eyes—then he toppled, falling backwards, slipping down the concrete steps until his head hit the pavement. Gary lay crumpled on the sidewalk, his leg bent at an awkward angle, blood pouring out of his head like red juice seeping from a cracked melon.

Lilly looked down from the top of the steps, her eyes triumphant. The implanted chip had fixed her moods, calmed her anger and bitterness after the divorce. But in the instant that Gary failed to shelter her from the rain, all her pent-up rage at men momentarily returned, resulting in her pushing him viciously away—exacting her ultimate revenge, killing him. It was an extreme reaction—a moment of deep, uncontrollable anger. She wondered, *was it a display of her chip gone bad or did it become an instrument to release her deepest desire, her dark evil within?*

The cab door was still open, the engine running, and the wipers going, not missing a beat. Lilly turned around, unlocked her front door, and walked inside, never looking back.

# Chapter 21

## DR. KITE

On the other side of town, Kite stood by his office window, watching the rain and the powerful storm raging outside. He preferred to be dry and inside on a day like this. No need to go out unless it was an emergency. From the comfort of his office, he watched the raindrops hitting the window and rolling down in steady streams. As a new drop flowed, it added to the stream, sometimes changing the course of it. He was so absorbed that he didn't hear the knock on the door. When the knock came again, this time louder and more insistent, he reluctantly turned around. "Come in."

Daman opened the door. He held a package in his hands. "New delivery, boss. This just came."

Kite could see it was stamped with the word *Urgent* in red letters. This was unusual. The delivery already came last Monday, and he wasn't expecting another one. He took the package quickly and ripped it open. He nodded dismissively to the kid, at the same time thanking him.

Inside the well-padded package was the usual black box.

However, this time a neatly typed note was attached to the outside of the box. It simply said, "Problem on Monday's package. Two out of three mind control chips defective."

Kite slowly closed the container. He stared at it, eyes wide open, as the horror started to sink in.

*Oh, God no. What have I done?*

# Chapter 22

## GIGI

Steve caught sight of the clock, irritably thinking, *Damn, it's getting late.* He had been so wrapped up in his work that time slipped by. All afternoon he had been watching the videotapes of the hotel parking garage. He poured over each one, checking the arrivals and departures of the vehicles to and from the parking deck, zooming in to see the drivers' and passengers' faces. It was a painstaking, slow process. He sat in his chair, frustrated and annoyed. By process of elimination, Steve ruled out the ones that didn't coincide with Gigi's arrival and cross-checked the rest against the roster of hotel guest's vehicles until he narrowed it down to a few. He wasn't able to see Gigi in any of the close-up frames of the inside of the vehicles. That didn't surprise him.

Rex had left Steve a voice mail to tell him they saw Gigi's car at the highway underpass before it was towed away, thanking him profusely. Steve felt a twinge of guilt that he hadn't had a chance to call him back. Perhaps it was better to wait until tomorrow. He may have more news then.

Steve stood up, holding the cup of cold, stale coffee in his hands. It was bad coffee to begin with. He had to be really desperate to drink that all afternoon. As a matter of fact, he didn't even have lunch. He made it through the day on coffee, candy, and junk food. A nice, hot home-cooked meal sounded very enticing now. But wait—he didn't have anyone at home waiting for him with a hot meal. He crushed the paper coffee cup and tossed it into the trash can along with the wrappers of his junk food. Tonight he would stop by the diner and treat himself to a nice meal.

Tomorrow would be another day.

# Chapter 23
## ELLEN

"I now pronounce you husband and wife. You may kiss the bride," said the pastor. The organ music filled the church as the exuberant couple dashed outside, the guests tossing pink flower petals for a sweet send-off.

Ellen wiped away a few happy tears. She wished with all her heart that one day she would find happiness like this to last a lifetime. And kids, well she loved kids, and wanted to start her own family soon.

She had buried this ache deep down inside her somewhere. She took solace with each bite, snuffing her dreams as the pounds and the inches crept up with each year that rolled by. She nursed every hurt and every pain with more food.

Food became the answer to everything. It was the healer, better than medicine. It was there at every occasion, every celebration. It was everywhere. Food became her interest, her necessity, and her obsession.

When she had an opportunity to choose, she chose food.

As she looked back on happy occasions when her friends and relatives celebrated weddings and births, every regret became replaced by food. Ellen didn't choose good food or bad food—it didn't matter. Food was what she could stuff in her mouth. It was sweet, it was spicy, it was salty, it was zesty. It was soft, it was crunchy, it was hard, it was solid, it was juicy.

It didn't matter.

She managed to lose some weight. She went on diets and worked so hard. Then she celebrated her success with food and gained back every pound that she'd lost. She did this again and again. And she noticed the older she got, the more easily she put on weight and the harder it was to lose it.

One day at work, she overheard some people making jokes about a fat woman when she stepped in the break room to microwave her lunch. Then she realized later they were talking about her. She was mortified. It was all she could do to make it through the day with her head held high. When she got home, she cried.

From that day forward, she watched every bite, counted calories, and managed to lose thirty-five pounds. She was determined to get her body back, and in the process, get her life back. She knew there had to be more to life than this— toiling away at the office, eating when she was upset, eating to take away the hurt. But the last thirty pounds were the hardest, and she couldn't get rid of them herself.

Kite had provided a lifeline. She took this new chance in life and grabbed it. Her time had come, and she was ready. This trip to her cousin's wedding was just the start. Grunting with satisfaction, Ellen replayed the clips in her mind—her

Mom left speechless (for once), her family and her cousin's family's stunned looks, and her friends' compliments at the wedding.

Ellen's thoughts turned to Brad on the plane. She really enjoyed herself, and the flirting came naturally. Men had always found her face attractive, and she retained her beauty and youthful appearance. But it had been a very long time since someone paid her much attention. When she saw him again, she would make up for lost time. She still had hopes that her life could be more than what it was today, the hope of love. No promises, no expectations, just taking life one day at a time. Who knows what could happen? Life is what it is.

A spark flew—that was for sure. And it wasn't just her. Ellen saw it in Brad's warm brown eyes, sensed he was just as interested in her as she was in him.

# Chapter 24

## GIGI

Rex noticed that Gigi was still a bit off. He had chalked it up to the trauma of the accident and her stress over it. He was worried about her and wanted to be sure that she wasn't going to go off the deep end or do something crazy. He checked in on her often while she was sleeping. Gigi had refused all medical treatments and insisted that she was all right. Rex didn't want to force her. If all she needed was time, time was what he would give her. Rex was a patient man. As he sat down with a cup of morning coffee, his cell phone rang.

"Hey Rex, got your message. How are you doing?"

"Oh, hey Steve. Man, I slept like a rock."

"And Gigi?"

"Slept through the night. I put a baby monitor in Gigi's room in case she woke up with another nightmare."

"So she's getting better?"

"Well, physically she is." He took a sip of his coffee. "I just hope her nightmares don't come back."

"Maybe it's time to take her to the doctor."

"She doesn't want to go yet. Hey, did you find out anything from the hotel parking cameras?"

"I was just about to update you on that," said Steve after a brief pause. "I've been able to narrow it down, and I'm checking the registrations now. My guess is one of these may lead to something. You're sure Gigi doesn't remember how she got to the hotel?"

"Not really. The only thing she said was she thought it was dark and she may have been lying down. She heard faint voices, but nothing that she could identify. And no details on the vehicles or anything else."

"Maybe she was blindfolded in the back, or in a van? If you find out anything else let me know."

"Yup, talk to you later."

Steve got back to his computer. There were two vehicles that he had questions about. The car tags on the camera didn't match the information in the system. The first vehicle was a black SUV. The owner's name and the registration showed a male and female with different last names.

He placed a call to the first person listed. "Hello, my name is Steve Cosine, and I'm a consultant looking into this. Your SUV popped up with a different name on the owner and the registration. Are you the owner?"

"What's this about? Am—am I in some kinda trouble?" said the guy who answered the phone.

"I'm trying to track down a vehicle that may have been involved in an accident. Is this your car?"

"We haven't gotten around to changing the information."

"So you are the owner?"

"*Was*—I got divorced and the wife, the ex-wife, well, she got the car."

"So you don't have the keys either?"

"I gave her the car when the divorce became final a few days ago, and that's when I gave her my keys. She was going to get the title changed to her name first."

"Were you driving the vehicle at the Hotel Seven or was it your ex-wife?"

"I didn't go there."

"Any reason for your ex-wife to be there?"

"Yeah, I think so. She's an event coordinator—books rooms, handles food, drinks, and all those details. You could easily confirm that with the hotel."

Satisfied, Steve concluded by saying, "This will do for now. Thanks for your cooperation."

Steve spoke with his contact at the hotel, and it all checked out.

Now, he skipped to the last name he had circled and put a question mark next to it. The vehicle was a white van registered in a man's name. He made a note of the address and decided to go in person to check it out. The location was in a dilapidated part of town, run-down and a little seedy. Steve knocked on the door. Hearing no sound, he pounded, this time much louder. He definitely heard something—voices, and the sound of chairs being pushed.

Finally, he heard a female voice and the door opened. "Hello," she said cautiously.

"I'm looking for Raul. Is he here?"

She looked over her shoulder and shouted, "Raul?"

An old man limped from the back room.

Steve held up a photo of the white van. "Is this your van?"

Raul's eyes lit up. "You found it?"

"Is this your van? Where is it?"

"I don't know. It looks like my white van, but it was stolen," stuttered Raul.

"Did you report it?"

Raul hesitated.

Maybe there was some reason he was holding back. Steve softened his voice. "Look, I'm not here to get you in trouble with the authorities. I just want to know about your vehicle. It may have been involved in an accident."

Raul relaxed and shook his head. But he insisted, "I don't know."

It was clear he didn't know who stole his vehicle, and he was too afraid to report it once it was stolen. Track this vehicle down and likely Steve would find the abductors.

# Chapter 25

## ELLEN

Ellen could hardly wait for the plane to land. She was so looking forward to coming home, and the thought of seeing Brad again made her feel like a giddy girl with a high school crush. An image of Brad popped up—a tall, handsome dude with a perfectly toned body and muscles that other men envied. Well, it took a *bit* of imagination seeing how Ellen had only seen him with his shirt on. Brad had texted her after the wedding, and they firmed up their plans to get together tonight for dinner. He was such a gentleman, insisting on picking her up. For a moment she wished he'd bring her a corsage and take her to the prom. She, Ellen, on Brad's arm. All eyes on them.

Ellen checked the clock on the dashboard while she was driving home from work. She had two and a half hours to get home, take a shower, and get ready. He said he'd be picking her up at 6:00 p.m. She had gotten off work a little early to avoid the rush-hour traffic, which was particularly bad on a Friday. She was able to whiz home in no time at all. After a quick shower, she put on a little red dress that she had picked up on the trip in anticipation of the date. It was tight-fitting and flattered her shape in all the right places. She was pleased.

Ellen heard the knock on the door. Brad was right on time. She took one last look at herself in the mirror, admiring the way her backside looked, before going to open the door.

"Well, *hello* Ellen." Brad gave a long whistle when he saw her.

Blushing, she gave him a quick welcoming hug. "Brad."

Brad held her for a second longer before releasing her.

"So, where're we going?" Ellen said.

"It's a surprise," he said with a laugh.

"I'm assuming you've got as much good taste in food as women?" she teased.

"I'll let you be the judge of that."

Ellen laughed heartily as they walked to his car, at ease with the banter.

The new seafood restaurant was the rave of town, and she had actually read the reviews. It was stunning, decorated in various tones of blue, all artfully done to give the impression that you were in an ocean—in the deep blue sea. At any moment, you almost expected to meet a mermaid or a school of fish. Stepping into the restaurant was like entering another world ruled by Neptune.

The food was delicious, skillfully prepared with the freshest of seafood. For starters, Ellen had the strawberry spinach salad with crumbled seaweed chips. Brad had the chilled shrimp cocktail with red chili cocktail sauce. For the entrée, hers was the restaurant's signature raw oysters with Russian caviar, his was the seared sea scallops with ginger lime sauce.

They took their time with the meal, stretching out the delightful evening. Ellen enjoyed every bit of it. After making their way through salad, appetizer, and the entrée, there was no room for dessert, so they ordered coffee and talked.

On the way back, as Brad drove, Ellen lay in the seat and almost purred. Brad turned to look at her. "That good, huh?"

"You weren't kidding about that place."

He grinned sheepishly. "And who said I have great taste?"

She pushed his arm playfully. "Take me home."

"At your service," he said with a salute.

They joked and teased all the way to her apartment.

Brad parked, got out, and went around to open her door for her.

Ellen thought, *every bit a gentleman.* "Would you like some dessert now?"

"If you're making good coffee…"

"Nothing but the best in this house," said Ellen as she turned the key. Brad was right behind her—his hand brushing against her arm when he reached out to hold the door open. She quivered at his touch, so light and electrifying.

As soon as they got inside, she slammed the door shut and kicked off her shoes. Brad moved closer and she stepped forward, her chin up, her lips parting slightly, her eyes beckoning as he searched for her response. Cupping her face in his hands, his lips brushed hers gently. She responded with a greater sense of urgency. They kissed passionately, lips locking. When they broke for air, he whispered hoarsely in her ear, "Are you my dessert?"

Laughing between kisses, she pushed him down the hallway to her bedroom, shedding her clothing along the way. They flopped on the bed, Brad on top. Ellen felt athletic, lithe, and free as she moved, swayed, and curved around Brad. His body matched hers, in movement and in playfulness. Ellen hooked her leg around Brad for leverage and flipped over easily. She became the lead, directing and guiding. They did a quick dance, passionate and playful.

As Ellen nuzzled his ear and tickled the hairs on his chest, moving down to between his legs and the really long curly hairs there, Brad groaned, his body announcing he was ready for another dance.

They started slowly this time, gently touching, exploring each other's body to find all the right steps and movements. He easily clasped his hands around her slim waist and lifted her up before positioning her on top. Soon they were both almost out of breath, reaching that final exquisite crescendo. At that moment, Ellen caught a glimpse of the time on her digital clock—8:30. Ellen was still on top, and Brad had his eyes closed—but in that instant, her body changed.

Brad clasped his hands around Ellen's waist again, but instead of a smooth, slim waist, his fingers grasped flesh—rolls of flesh like dough that he could dig his fingers into.

His mind refused to comprehend what his hands were telling him. As his part shriveled and his head started to clear, Brad kept his eyes closed as he moved his hands slowly up and down her back. He stopped, freezing at her butt. He slowly flattened his palms, expanding his fingers as wide as they could go, first to one side, then the other, measuring the span of her butt in disbelief.

Ellen was in pure ecstasy when they reached the crescendo together. She almost lost her mind. But in that same instant, as her whole body quaked in tandem with Brad's—it changed. With a sickening feeling, she felt her body expand and become heavy. Heavy like she gained back the thirty pounds she had lost and more.

# Chapter 26

## GIGI

When she finally remembered, Gigi knew why she'd rather be dead. It became all too clear to her. The events of the past few days were no longer a void.

Gigi had a condition, tinnitus, a ringing and sometimes a buzzing sound in her ears. At first, she tried to ignore it as the noise came and went intermittently, albeit occasionally at the most inconvenient or embarrassing circumstances.

She tried to live with it, managing it as it appeared, hiding it from people. Gradually, the sounds became louder, more persistent, and present for longer periods of time. Day and night, the noise in her head affected her waking and sleeping hours, keeping her up most of the night.

Tortured by her condition, Gigi sought out doctors, but they could never find the cause. She tried their treatments. Some temporarily masked the symptoms or provided limited relief, but none could cure this condition. She couldn't get the noise out of her head, and feared she would go crazy living with this.

Frantic, out of options, and desperate, she heard through the grapevine about a doctor who was whispered to be quite unconventional and secretive. She arranged for a visit through contacts and was picked up by Kite's cab driver at a predestined location. Then she was blindfolded and taken to see Kite, where he swore her to secrecy before implanting the first-generation microchip. It was her last-ditch effort after everything she tried had failed. She was determined not to give up.

She went back to see Kite last Monday after he received the new shipment, and he replaced her original microchip with an upgraded one. That was in the morning. Her terrifying nightmares started that night, then the car accident a few days later.

Gigi had blocked out the trauma of the accident. She dreaded reliving it, not wanting to face the truth. The new nightmares had been real. They were as much a part of her life as anything. She couldn't even begin to describe the terror and the depth of pull she felt. Every waking hour she dreaded the nights. She tried to fight it as hard as she could, thinking, *I could beat it.* But as time went on, the nightmares and the pull to the other side became stronger and stronger, until it reached a crescendo—as her car hurled toward the concrete wall.

In the last few months, it became clear to her how much Rex meant to her. He was her comforter, protector, best friend, the person she'd call if she had one last call to make. Rex stuck with her, helping her to cope and deal with her illness. Her whole life changed with the tinnitus, but having him there made all the difference.

Seeing his actions throughout this ordeal and realizing the very essence of his soul stirred something deep inside her—at the instant when it mattered, as she confronted the fragility of life and released the courage that was within her.

His love gave her the strength to live, and she fought to survive. But now she wanted more, and with the tinnitus and nightmares gone, she was ready. She needed to tell Rex, and he needed to hear the truth now. She picked up her pen.

*My dear Rex—I **never** gave up. What I can tell you is how it felt, like a switch had been turned and my time was up. My body went through the motions and I couldn't stop it. It was as if I was on autopilot. The near-crash was no accident. I was headed toward the wall, a certain death.*

*I can't explain why it didn't happen except to say that at the last moment a part of me wouldn't surrender to it and, with every bit of fierce strength that I had left, I somehow wrenched the wheel, changing the path. A few days before, the new nightmares came with an intensity and depth that was more frightening than any I've ever experienced. I didn't want to fall down the precipice to the darkness below. I tried so hard to fight it. You were by my side. But each day, the pull became stronger and stronger, bringing me closer to the wall, right up to the accident.*

*I've got a second chance to live now. Perhaps one day
we'll be lovers. I'd like that.*
*Gigi*

# Chapter 27

## DR. KITE

Kite looked up as the light blinked during the storm. He sighed, rubbing his eyes. The defect in two of the three chips was a cruel twist. He didn't know for sure who had received those. He shook his head. Wearily, he entered a comment in the system for each of the three names—Gigi, Ellen, Lilly: INAPPROPRIATE SUBJECT FOR IMPLANTS. REMOVE DEFECTIVE UPGRADE CHIP.

He had replaced Gigi's chip already. Reaching for his cell phone, it rang before he could make a call to arrange the other removals.

"Hello?"

"Warehouse burning…" said the other man on the line.

"*What?* Say that again!"

"Burned… struck by lightning."

"No, oh no!" said Kite repeatedly as he listened to catch every word uttered by the frantic, blubbering man on the other end.

"Called 911?"

"Yeah, line was flooded."

"Did you try calling the fire department?"

"Couldn't get through in time, fire trucks out…"

"In the storm?"

"Got here too late…"

Kite tapped his cell phone abruptly, ending the call in mid-sentence. All of his work, destroyed. He gripped the phone, wanting to throw it, to smash it into smithereens.

# Chapter 28
## LILLY

The storm that took the city wreaked havoc and left devastation in its path. The governor had declared a state of emergency. Sirens could be heard wailing most of the day. The exhausted fire and police were stretched thin. Volunteers helped in the rescue. In the hours that transpired, the death of Gary was counted as another casualty of the storm. Lilly was questioned and released. There were no witnesses.

# Epilogue

## A YEAR LATER

# Chapter 29

## ELLEN

*Knock, knock.*

"Mom, thanks for coming over tonight," said Ellen, opening her door.

Brushing a kiss on Ellen's cheek as she walked in, her mom was carrying a large green tote. "I picked up some groceries on the way."

"I couldn't have done it alone without your help these last three months."

"That's why your dad and I moved down here, Elly."

"Yeah, and I am so glad you did—*Grandma.*"

Walking to the nursery, Grandma pulled out the newest toy she had brought, a soft puffamuffin penguin. Chuckling to the baby in the crib, she reached in with a practiced hand. "Now let me hold my little Angie."

"Mom," said Ellen as she leaned over to tuck in a corner of the blanket, making sure Angie was snuggly wrapped. "I'm so happy now... so thoroughly in love with my baby."

"She's so beautiful."

"Angie's the best thing that's ever happened to me, and I have Brad to thank for it."

"I thought… isn't Brad's out of the picture? You're a single mom now."

"Yes, but if it wasn't for him I wouldn't have Angie."

"Well, you sure know how to pick them. She's got his genes and good looks too."

"I did something else right this time," said Ellen as she smoothed her hands down her size eight slacks. After she got over the shock that followed the last scene with Brad, when her weight instantly jumped back up and then she found out she was pregnant, Ellen channeled all her determination into transforming her body, not just for herself but also for the new life she was carrying. She started small, cutting out bread, sugary snacks, and sodas. She ate healthy meals but smaller portions. She cut out meats and fried foods. She ate folate-rich foods. She walked a lot and did prenatal workouts. She changed her attitude. There was no going back once she started, fueled with new life and her energy.

"Are those new pants?"

"Yeah, Mom. I'm down another size and have kept my weight off since I had Angie. I did it this time, my way."

"I'm so proud of you— Ellen!"

"You just keep calling me Ellen. I hate it when you call me Elly."

"I'm sorry…"

"Forget the past. Elly is gone."

"I've never seen you happier."

"I know, Mom, *I know*."

# Chapter 30

## LILLY

*Knock, knock.*

Lilly was in the kitchen making a pot of fresh coffee when she heard the knock. She glanced up at the clock. It was 10:00 a.m., and she wasn't expecting anyone. *Who could it be?* With a sigh of irritation, she snatched a towel and quickly wiped her hands dry.

*"Be just a minute,"* she yelled.

Opening the door, she found a stranger standing on her doorstep. It was a man dressed in a frumpy shirt with a slightly crooked tie.

"Excuse me," the man said, as he straightened his tie with one hand. "Are you Mrs. Cooper?"

She gave him her cool look, accompanied with a cooler and somewhat imperious tone as she demanded, "And who is asking?"

He cleared his throat. "Ma'am, I'm Steve Cosine. I'm a consultant on an insurance investigation."

"You must have the wrong house," she said, ready to slam the door in his face.

"Hold it," he said, shoving his foot in the doorstep. "You are Lilly Cooper, right?"

She barely nodded.

"You can talk to me now, or I can call the detective to re-open the case." He held up his cell phone. "I know who to call. I'm retired from the force. Now which shall it be?"

She glared at him defiantly. "I'm not going to let you in the house."

"I don't have to come in. We can talk here." Putting his phone back in his pocket, he pulled out a small notepad and pen. "Now Mrs. Cooper, I just need to ask you a few questions." He flipped to a page. "Where were you on the day of the storm?"

She shrugged and scowled. "Now, how am I supposed to know, just whip that date out of my memory bank?"

"Perhaps I can help jog your memory? The really big storm a year ago. You remember that?"

"Oh, the one that downed power lines and caused a lot of destruction… who can forget that?"

"Well, Mrs. Cooper, if you would just remember that storm, I'd like to get more specific information on where you were and what you were doing." Steve looked up, waiting

"I suppose I was here, waiting out the storm like a lot of people."

"I get that, but were you out at any time that day, perhaps earlier, before it got really bad?"

She looked at him, but didn't answer.

Steve pressed her, "Mrs. Cooper, do you know someone named Gary?"

"Gary?"

"Yes, Gary. Who drives a taxi."

She felt a shiver run up her spine as realization slowly dawned on her. Still, she shook her head. "I'm afraid I don't know who you are talking about."

"Let me refresh your memory. The day of the storm, Gary, the taxi driver, was found dead outside, right in front of your home."

"The police have already questioned me. Why are you here?"

"I'm hired by the insurance company. You see, his life insurance policy covered death due to natural and accidental causes... but there was an exclusion clause."

"I don't understand..."

"According to the exclusion clause, we withhold payment in the case of a homicide."

He pulled out his card and handed it to her. "Mrs. Cooper, if you happen to remember anything, just give me a call. My phone number and email are both on the card. Anytime. You call me, okay?"

She nodded, afraid to speak, fearing the growing weakness in her voice would betray her this time. He withdrew his foot as she closed her door. She pressed her back against it, partly to hold it in place and partly to steady herself. Shaking slightly, she walked back to the kitchen and started the coffee.

She sat at the counter with her fresh cup, nursing the warm mug, her mind going back to that day. She had repelled all thoughts of what happened and, as time went on, it became easier to forget, to pretend that it had never taken place. Gary, so that was his name. She had never asked him.

Early on, Lilly had worried about the incident. She had convinced herself that it was an accident and blamed it on the weather. At that time, storm-related incidents were happening all over the city. No one had witnessed anything or come forth with any accusations. She simply assumed that they had forgotten about it, closing the book on it in the craziness that happened during and in the aftermath of the storm.

Now it had come back to haunt her after all this time. Lilly couldn't believe it. It was almost a year ago and they *hadn't* forgotten. Lilly forced herself to stay calm, to think. What if they didn't believe her this time? She repeated her thoughts, *There were no witnesses. It was just an accident.*

Steve knew something was off with Lilly Cooper. He didn't know exactly what yet. The operative word was *yet*. So it was just a matter of time until he got to the truth of the matter. Catching her off guard, when she least expected it.

He was a patient man. People get careless. They get forgetful. Or people get impatient. Or scared. They trip up somehow, they always do. They think they are smart, smarter than anyone out there.

# Chapter 31

## GIGI

Gigi turned her head, nuzzling his cheek as she whispered, "Good night."

He still had his eyes closed, but a grin spread across his face. "No more nightmares, right?"

"Nope… nothing since that awful accident."

Reaching to pull her closer, Rex opened his eyes, showing the love in them, gazing at her face as if to etch it in his mind forever. "Gigi…"

Gigi smiled and moved closer, resting her head partially on his pillow.

His finger gently traced the curves of her upper lip to the edge, and around to her bottom. He murmured, "I love you" before planting a tender, sweet kiss on her lips.

# Acknowledgments

I want to first thank my family and friends for their love and support over the years. When the going got tough, they've kept me going. I love you.

Thanks to my beta readers and editors Graeme Hague, Deborah Dove, Marina Anderson and Jason Anderson at Polgarus Studios and everyone who has been part of this book.

# Author's note

Thank you for reading "Alterations". I hope you enjoyed this story. I've benefited from the feedback that I've received from readers since the publication of my award-winning debut novel. If you have time to write a review, whether it's long or a few words, know that I will read it. Please review on the site where you got the book.

CPSIA information can be obtained
at www.ICGtesting.com
Printed in the USA
LVOW11s1307030817

543705LV00001B/8/P